Dear Eduard
"I love you!"
– MMe

First published in Belgium and Holland by Clavis Uitgeverij, Hasselt – Amsterdam, 2014
Copyright © 2014, Clavis Uitgeverij

English translation from the Dutch by Clavis Publishing Inc. New York
Copyright © 2015 for the English language edition: Clavis Publishing Inc. New York

Visit us on the web at www.clavisbooks.com

I See, I see written by Pimm van Hest and illustrated by Nynke Talsma
Original title: *Ik zie, ik zie*
Translated from the Dutch by Clavis Publishing

ISBN 978-1-60537-247-1

This book was printed in September 2015 at Publikum d.o.o., Slavka Rodica 6, Belgrade, Serbia

First Edition
10 9 8 7 6 5 4 3 2 1

I See, I See

Pimm van Hest & Nynke Talsma

Clavis

NEW YORK

"You need glasses!"

Edward jumps.
He moves a bit closer to Mom.
"You have trouble seeing everything
in detail now, but with glasses you'll have eyes
that are as sharp as an eagle's!"
The doctor leans forward, stares at Edward,
and pretends his arms are wings.

Edward feels like a little mouse
that's about to be eaten.
When he opens his mouth,
all that comes out is a small squeak.
Poor Edward.
His eyes fill with tears,
and he can hardly see the doctor.
Maybe that's for the best.

That night Edward dreams he is a little mouse.
Wearing glasses.
If you see Mister Mole wearing glasses, that's okay.
No one will think it odd.
Or Miss Cat,
who is one hundred years old and gray.
Everyone understands that.
But a young mouse wearing glasses?
Everyone will laugh at him.

The next morning Edward is even more worried.
"I don't want glasses,"
he says out loud to himself,
but when he looks in the mirror
while brushing his teeth,
he sees two sad little eyes,
and they do want glasses, badly.

That afternoon
Edward goes to the glasses store
with his parents.
"What kind of glasses would you like?"
the friendly lady asks.
Edward looks at the floor.
"Do you happen to have
transparent glasses?" he asks quietly.
Mom and Dad laugh,
but the saleslady doesn't.

She kneels down in front of him
and lifts up his chin.
"I understand that this is pretty scary for you.
But can I tell you a secret?"
She bends forward and whispers in his ear:
"With glasses you will see things
that other people don't.
Special things.
Just wait and see."

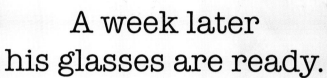

A week later
his glasses are ready.
Edward is still a bit scared,
but he is also a bit curious.
"Are you ready for the big moment?"
the kind lady from the store asks.
Edward nods and closes his eyes.
She stands in front of him
and carefully puts the glasses on his nose.
Very carefully he opens his eyes.

Deep down he had expected fireworks
and bright colors and WOW!
and KABOOM!
But that doesn't happen.
Everything looks just the same.

Except....

When he blinks again,
he sees something sparkle on the carpet.
While the adults talk about bills
and cloths for cleaning glasses,
Edward disappears underneath the desk.

There he sees a shiny ring.
He is so excited that he bumps
his head when he stands up.
"My wedding ring!?"
the lady from the store says.
"You found my wedding ring!"
She is so happy that she gives him
three big lipstick kisses.

Edward blushes and smiles...
**and adjusts the glasses
on his nose.**

Outside, Dad says, "It's time to play a game.
I spy with my little eye… a pigeon in his nest."
Edward looks at all the trees.
He sees the veins in the beautiful green leaves.
He's never seen those before.
He also sees the pigeon in the nest.

Sale

"Over there!" he yells. "There!
Up in that tree. Now it's my turn," Edward says happily.
"I spy with my little eye… a sign that reads *Sale*."
Mom and Dad scan the store windows,
but they don't see it.

"Over there!" Edward points with his finger.
"Oh, but I can't read that from this distance, sweetheart,"
says Dad, somewhat taken aback.
"Do you want to borrow my glasses?" Edward asks.
All three of them burst out laughing.

That night before Edward goes to sleep,
Mom and Dad sit on his bed.
Dad has taken a pile of *I Spy* books from the shelves.
They aren't Edward's favorite books.
It's no fun if you can never find anything.

But today he's wearing glasses.

"I see it, Dad! There is the yellow balloon,
between the branches of the tree.
And over there and there and there and there.
And look, Mom, there is a mouse with a cake,
and here's the fly wearing a party hat."
Never before has Edward seen so much,
and never before has he had so much fun.
He goes to bed with a smile on his face.

Edward wakes up in the middle of the night.
He turns over and suddenly he sees something
in the corner of his room.
Is it a monster?
As quick as lightning he pulls the covers over his head.
His heart is thumping.
What should he do?

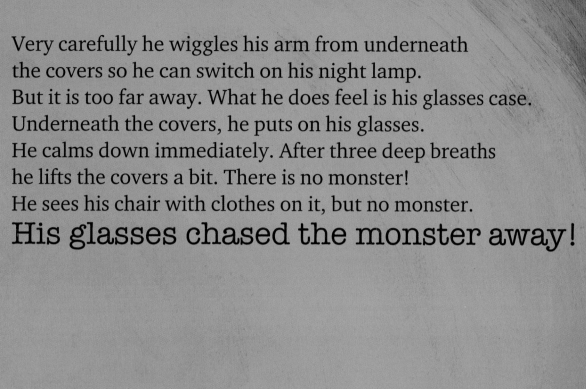

Very carefully he wiggles his arm from underneath
the covers so he can switch on his night lamp.
But it is too far away. What he does feel is his glasses case.
Underneath the covers, he puts on his glasses.
He calms down immediately. After three deep breaths
he lifts the covers a bit. There is no monster!
He sees his chair with clothes on it, but no monster.
His glasses chased the monster away!

When Edward walks to school the next day,
it seems as if the world has changed.
He sees all sorts of things he hadn't noticed before.
A loose paving stone, the numbers on the church clock,
and even the ants that walk to school with him.
He loves it. He watches a ladybug fly through the sky.
After a while he loses the bug.

But what is it he sees now?

Not the boring white clouds he used to see before.
Now they have turned into knights who are being
chased by a fire-breathing dragon. Farther along
he sees his name in the clouds, and near the school
he sees a smiling mouse with glasses on its nose.

A few moments later, when she is working
in her notebook, he looks at her carefully.
She has beautiful freckles on her cheek.
He has never noticed them.
And that cute tip-tilted nose has never
caught his eye before.
It makes his tummy tickle.

At school Edward doesn't have to sit by himself all the way in the front of the class.
The teacher puts him in a seat next to Linda.
"You have such beautiful glasses,"
Linda says to him.
"Th-th-thank you," Edward stammers nervously.

"You ll see special things with glasses,"

the lady from the store had told him. She was right!
And to top it off, Linda liked his glasses.
Edward feels as if he's grown ten inches
since he got the glasses.

At the end of the school day
he gathers his courage,
walks over to Linda, straightens his glasses,
and without stammering he asks her:
"Do you want to walk home with me?"

"I would love to!" Linda says.

Edward and Linda look at the clouds.
"I see a giant stumbling
over a tree trunk."
"Yes, I see it too!"
"And over there I see a volcano erupting.
And a roller coaster going upside down."
They see all sorts of things and have a lot of fun.

Then Linda says,
"I see a boy who gets a kiss from a girl
who really likes him."
"Oh," says Edward, "I don't see that."
He searches the clouds,
but no matter how hard he looks,
he can't see it.

"Maybe you're looking in the wrong place," Linda says,
and when Edward turns his head toward her,
she gives him a kiss on the cheek.
The kiss makes him all warm inside.

From that day on Linda is his girlfriend.

Now you see what **a difference a pair of glasses** can make....